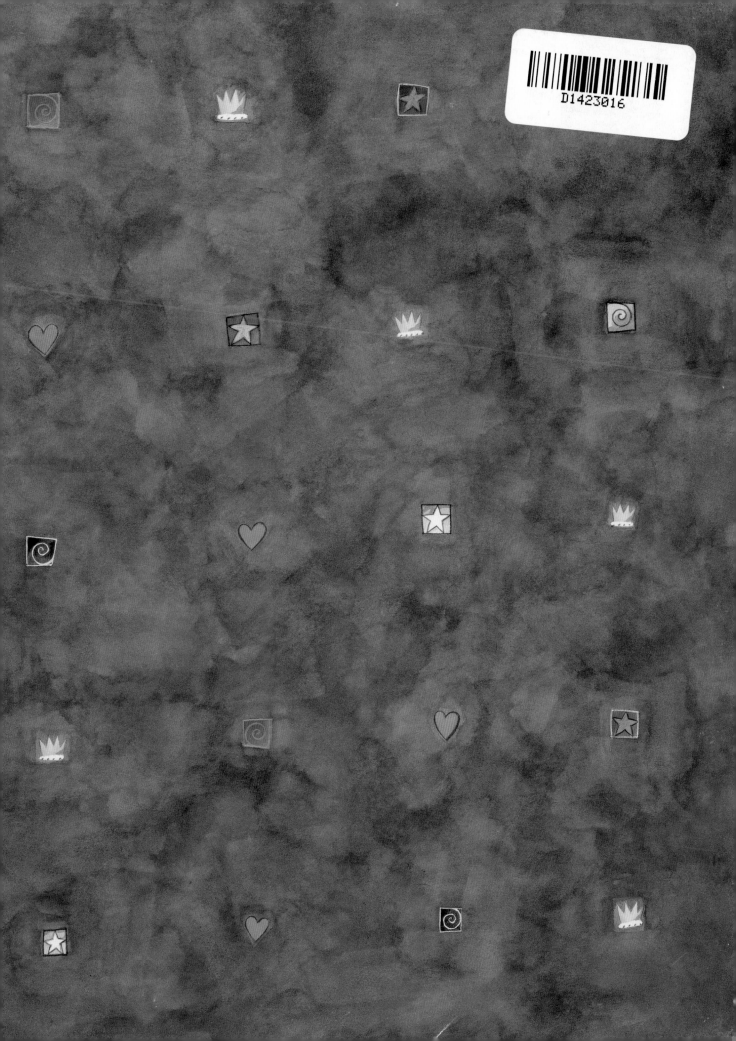

D1423016

Hidden Tales from Eastern Europe copyright © Frances Lincoln Limited 2002
Text copyright © Antonia Barber 2002
Illustrations copyright © Paul Hess 2002

**The publishers would like to thank Gabriela Kianickova
for sourcing and translating the stories**

First published in Great Britain in 2002 by
Frances Lincoln Limited, 4 Torriano Mews
Torriano Avenue, London NW5 2RZ

www.franceslincoln.com

All rights reserved

No part of this publication may be reproduced, stored in a retrieval
system, or transmitted, in any form, or by any means, electrical,
mechanical, photocopying, recording or otherwise without
the prior written permission of the publisher or a licence
permitting restricted copying. In the United Kingdom
such licences are issued by the Copyright Licensing Agency,
90 Tottenham Court Road, London W1P 9HE.

British Library Cataloguing in Publication Data
available on request

ISBN 0-7112-1949-4

Set in Minion

Printed in Singapore
1 3 5 7 9 8 6 4 2

Some tradition for Stan and Leon (and mum e dad)!
love from Hugo, Wilbri, Adam, Gideon.

Hidden Tales
from Eastern Europe

RETOLD BY Antonia Barber

ILLUSTRATED BY Paul Hess

EDITED BY Shena Guild

FRANCES LINCOLN

For Jenni – A.B.

For my parents – S.G.

Contents

The Twelve Months

Slovakia

In a land where the summers are sweet and the winters harsh, there was once a young girl named Marushka. She lived with her stepmother, who would often beat her, while her own daughter, Holena, she petted and spoiled. Marushka had to work every hour of the day while Holena sat about, stuffing herself with sweetmeats.

As the years passed, Marushka grew very beautiful, while greedy Holena became fat and pasty-faced. This made the stepmother anxious. "Who will marry Holena," she thought, "if my pretty stepdaughter is around?" So she plotted with Holena to bring about Marushka's death.

They waited until winter and then Holena said, "Go out on to the mountainside, sister, and bring me back some violets."

Marushka was astonished. "Violets in January?" she asked.

"Do as I say!" shouted Holena. "I am tired of winter and I must have violets."

The stepmother joined in, and together they drove Marushka out into the snow, warning her that if she returned without the violets, she would find the door barred against her.

Setting out through the forest, Marushka made her way up to the mountain meadows where violets bloomed in spring. But all lay hidden now under a cold white blanket. As the light faded, the cold grew bitter and Marushka began to fear that she would not live to see the morning.

Then she saw a faint light and struggling towards it, beheld a strange sight. In a mountain hollow a great bonfire blazed and around it, lit by the flickering flames, stood a circle of stones. Upon them sat silent figures wrapped and hooded in grey, of whom only one could be clearly seen: an old man with a white beard and a noble face. He sat on a stone

shaped like a great throne and held a tall and wonderfully-carved staff.

Marushka was frightened by the silent figures, but feeling desperate, she approached the old man, saying politely, "Give me leave, good sir, to warm myself by your fire."

Slowly he turned his head towards her. "What brings you to this secret place?" he asked, and his voice was like the grinding of ice upon a frozen river.

Marushka told him how she had been sent to gather violets.

"No violets bloom while January rules," the old man told her.

"Then my home is lost to me," said Marushka, "and I shall die out in the cold."

When he heard this, the old man rose to his feet and stepped down from the throne. "Come, sister April," he called, "and bring violets in your path!"

One of the hooded figures rose and threw off its cloak. Marushka saw a sweet-faced girl, who took her place on the high throne.

The old man handed her the staff. Then April stretched out her hand, passing the staff above the fire. As she did so, the air grew warm, the snows melted, and amid the green grass there were violets everywhere.

"Take what flowers you will," said April, "but tell no one how you came by them."

"Oh, thank you, sweet April," breathed Marushka. Swiftly she gathered the tiny flowers, but before her hands were full, January had returned to the high throne and snow began to fall once more.

Marushka hurried home and knocked on the door. Holena appeared at the window. "What do you want?" she scowled.

"I have brought the violets," said Marushka.

At once the door was flung open and the violets were snatched from her hands.

"Where did you get them?" demanded her stepsister.

"In a sheltered valley high in the mountains," said Marushka.

Holena and her mother marvelled at the winter violets, but they were not pleased that Marushka had come safely home.

A few days passed, and then Holena sent her out again, this time to fetch wild strawberries.

My only hope, thought Marushka, is to find the Twelve Months, and she set out into the forest. Snow was falling and the way was hard, but at last she saw the light ahead and came to the stone circle.

"What brings you back to us?" asked January.

"My stepsister has a craving for strawberries," said Marushka, "and I may not go home without them."

January sighed, and his sigh was like the roar of the winter wind. "Come, brother July," he called, "and bring the first fruits of the harvest!"

From beneath his grey cloak came a young man, his smiling face crowned with the fruits of summer. Seating himself on the throne, he took the magic staff and passed it over the flames. The air grew warm, the snow vanished and the grass was starred with tiny wild strawberries.

"Gather them quickly," said July, and Marushka lost no time, filling her apron with the sweet red fruits. She thanked him and hurried away down the mountainside.

When Holena saw the strawberries she could hardly believe her eyes, but she snatched them away and gobbled up every one.

A few more days went by, and Holena had a new craving. She sent her stepsister out again to find fresh apples.

Marushka's heart was heavy as she came into the firelit circle, for she was afraid that she might trouble the Twelve Months once too often. January turned his white head towards her.

"Forgive me," said Marushka, "but there is no end to my stepsister's demands. Now I must find fresh apples, if I am not to perish in the snow."

January frowned, and his frown was like the darkness of a winter nightfall. Marushka trembled. But once more he rose up, and this time he called to October.

A buxom woman with rosy cheeks appeared from under her grey cloak. She sat on the high throne and passed the staff over the fire. The snow melted, and on the trees around the circle apples grew red and ripened.

"Shake the tree, child," said October, "and take whatever falls."

Marushka shook the tree, but she was not very strong and only two apples fell to the ground. It seemed greedy to shake the tree again, so she

picked up the two apples, and thanking October, made her way homeward.

When Holena saw only two apples, she grabbed them both and bit first into one and then into the other.

"Is this all you have brought me?" she demanded, spitting pips all over the floor.

"I shook the tree," said Marushka, "but only two apples came down."

"Liar!" shouted Holena. "You have eaten the others yourself!"

She seized a broom and began to beat her stepsister. Her mother came in and hearing Holena's story, joined her in beating poor Marushka.

Then Holena said, "I will go myself and bring back a whole basketful of apples. Marushka's tracks are clear in the snow and I shall soon find this secret valley."

"And you shall not go alone, my love," said her mother. "I will go with you to see that you come safely home."

The stepmother and Holena followed Marushka's footprints until they reached the circle of stones. Ignoring the old man, they warmed themselves at the fire, talking loudly about Marushka and the apples, strawberries and violets.

"The footprints end here, but there is no sheltered valley," said Holena angrily. And the stepmother said, "She shall pay dearly for her lies!"

Then January spoke. "What brings you to this place?" he asked, and his voice had the threatening roar of a winter avalanche.

"What business is that of yours, old fool?" said Holena rudely, and she went on talking to her mother in her harsh, ugly voice.

Then January's face grew dark. Raising his staff, he passed it over the fire and at once the flames died. A fierce wind came moaning down

from the mountain heights and a blizzard fell from the sky.

Frightened now, Holena turned to go home and her mother followed. But already the tracks were vanishing beneath the blinding snow. So thick did it fall that before long they could not see their hands in front of their faces.

It may be that they stumbled from the path and fell into a crevasse, or perhaps they were buried by the deep snowfall. For neither Holena nor her mother was ever seen again.

Below, in the farmhouse, Marushka waited patiently. When they did not return, she lit a lantern to go in search of them. But the snowfall had covered the whole house in a white drift, blocking both windows and doors. Days passed before she could get out, and when she did, she found no trace of them.

Winter passed and the snows melted. When April came bringing violets and July followed with sweet strawberries, Marushka welcomed them as old friends.

Summer turned to autumn and October came, bringing with her a handsome young man. He worked the travelling cider-press but, falling in love with Marushka, stayed with her to work the land. In time they were married and had children of their own.

Marushka proved a wise and gentle mother. She taught her children that as the months pass, each one, from hottest July to coldest January, comes to us in its own way as a blessing and a friend.

Misery

Poland

In a land far away, there once lived a rich man in a fine mansion and a poor man who dwelt in a hovel nearby. The rich man lived well, but his neighbour's life was hard and wretched, for Misery lived in his house.

Misery sat in the chimney corner. He made the poor man's fire smoke and burn low so that his house was never warm. Misery sat at the poor man's table and breathed upon his food, so that what little meat he had was tough and tasteless. Worst of all, Misery slept in the poor man's bed between him and his wife, so that they turned their backs upon one another and shivered under the thin blankets.

Then one spring morning, the wife looked out at the earth newly waking and the flowers coming into bloom. She thought, our life would not be so very bad if only Misery did not live with us! So she spoke kindly to her husband and asked him if they could find some way to drive Misery out.

Her husband was touched by her words, and he sat and thought. Then he went into his woodshed and picked up a wide plank of wood. He called to his wife and together they set out into the wild wood.

After they had walked some way, the man looked back and saw Misery following them. They reached a deep stream and the husband put down the plank for his wife to walk across. Quickly he followed her, pulling up the plank before Misery could reach it. But when he glanced back again, he saw that Misery had moved a huge tree trunk so that he could cross the stream, and was still following behind.

The poor man knew of an old hollow tree deep in the wood. When he reached it, he put down the plank, cut a branch from the tree and began to shape some wooden wedges. Misery came closer to see what he was doing.

"I can't stand living with Misery any longer," the man said loudly to his wife. "I am going to shut myself up in this hollow tree where he can never get at me again. You must drive in the wedges, Wife, to hold the plank fast and keep him out."

"I will do it, Husband," said the wife, for she saw that her husband was setting a trap.

Misery could not bear to see the poor man escape him, so at the last moment he sprang into the hollow tree, just as the man was climbing in. At once the man jumped out again, and with his wife's help put the plank in place and drove the wedges home. When it was done, the poor man and his wife looked at one another and laughed for the first time in many years.

With Misery gone, the couple walked home hand in hand, and it seemed that already their luck was changing, for they found a purse with some gold coins lying in the road.

Soon the poor man's house was a very different place. The fire burned brightly, the food tasted good. And with Misery gone from their bed, the poor man and his wife kept one another warm and slept well at night. The vegetables in their garden flourished and they had enough to sell

at market. The hens laid more eggs and soon they made enough money to buy a pig. The wife sang as she swept the house clean. With Misery gone, life was worth living at last.

But the man was still afraid that Misery might escape from the hollow tree and come back to plague them. So each week he went to the tree to make sure that the wedges were still tight. And if any seemed loose, he would hammer them in again.

Now, the rich man had noticed how his poor neighbour prospered. He has found some treasure, he thought, and he goes into the wood each week to take a little more gold from his store. So the next time the poor man went into the wood, the rich man followed him.

Watching from the bushes, he saw the poor man hammering away at the wedges.

"Ah," thought the rich man, "so that is where he keeps his treasure!" Although he was wealthy, he was always greedy for more gold. He waited until the poor man had gone and quickly knocked out the wedges to see what was hidden in the hollow tree … And at once Misery leapt out!

He was so pleased to be free that he followed the rich man home, and from that day lived in his house instead. For riches are no guard against Misery. It takes love and kindness, and sometimes a little cunning, to keep Misery at bay.

The Shepherd King

Serbia

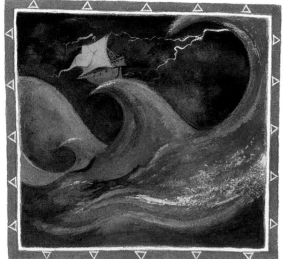

A king once set sail on a fine summer day to visit another kingdom. He took with him his young daughter, so that she might learn from his example how royal folk behave on a state visit. As they sailed across the blue-green seas, he told her of the ceremonies that would greet them on their arrival and the part she must play in them.

But even the plans of kings can go astray. As they sat talking, dark clouds were gathering on the far horizon. The sun went in, the sea turned grey, and the wind blew with the force of a hurricane, driving the ship far away from its intended course. Soon the sails were ripped to shreds, the masts toppled, and it was clear that the ship would founder.

The sailors could do nothing to save their king and princess, but lash them with ropes to a floating mast and hope that the tides would carry them to some friendly shore. Half-drowned, and fearing death at every moment, the king and his daughter slipped into unconsciousness as the storm passed.

When the princess opened her eyes, she was lying on a sandy beach with the body of her father close by. Untying the ropes, she crawled to his side and found with joy that he still breathed. She went in search of fresh water and, bathing his sunburned face and moistening his cracked lips, she brought him back to life.

His tired face lit up with joy when he saw her. But looking about him, he said, "Alas! my daughter. I fear the lessons I taught you on the voyage will be of little use to you here."

The princess found fruit and berries for them to eat and when the king was strong enough to stand, they went in search of shelter. Hearing sheep-bells in the far distance, they made their way towards the sound and came at last upon a hut where shepherds were cooking their dinner over an open fire. The smell was so inviting that the king took his daughter by the hand and led her into the clearing.

"Good people," he said, "we are poor wretches shipwrecked upon your shore, with nothing but the rags we stand up in. Give us, I beg you, some little share in your food." The princess thought how strange it was to hear her father beg, when in their own land their every need had always been provided for.

The shepherds were kindly folk and made them welcome. After they had eaten, the king asked where they had come ashore. To his dismay, he learned that it was a land unfriendly to his own kingdom because of an old quarrel. So he decided to tell no one that he was a king or his daughter a princess. And in any case, he thought, with our sunburned faces and torn, ragged clothes, who would believe us?

Instead, he gladly accepted the shepherds' offer of work caring for the flocks. It was hard labour, with never a day's rest, but at least it gave them food and shelter. The princess worked too, caring for motherless lambs and learning to spin fleeces and weave cloth. In this new life there was nothing to be had without working for it.

At night, as they sat around the fire keeping watch against wolves, the shepherds would dream of the good lives they might have led if they had learned a trade.

"If only I had been a carpenter," one would say; and another: "The blacksmith's trade pays even better," and a third: "A potter would be my choice."

"Could you not learn these skills and change your lives?" asked the king. The shepherds shook their heads sadly. "It takes years to learn a trade," they told him, "and how could we live in the meantime?"

"I wish I had learned a trade myself," said the king to the princess, when they were alone together. "Then I could provide for you properly."

The princess tried to comfort him. "But is not

kingship a trade, Father?" she asked. "It takes many years to learn to rule wisely and well."

The king sighed. "If kingship is indeed a trade," he said, "I fear it is not much in demand."

So it was that the king remained a humble shepherd.

The years passed, until his daughter was of an age to marry. Now, for all her rough clothes and sun-tanned face, the princess had grown into a young woman of great beauty, and one day she was seen by the prince of that land when he came hunting among the hills. The memory of her face stayed with him, and he found himself again and again taking the path that led to the sheepfold. When at last he spoke to the shepherd girl, the prince found that her voice was soft and her manner gentle. Soon he fell deeply in love with her.

The prince went back to his father's palace and told him that he wished to marry a shepherd girl. The king and queen were horrified and begged him to think again, but the prince said that if he could not wed the shepherd girl, he would stay single all his life. So the king and queen sent a carriage and brought the young woman to the palace to see her for themselves.

When she came, they were charmed by her sweet voice and pleasant ways. Seeing how their son's face lit up whenever she was near, they gave in at last and consented to the marriage.

"You must send counsellors to ask for her father's approval," said the prince.

"Well, he will hardly refuse!" laughed the king. "But you are right: it is a necessary courtesy."

So it was that a party of counsellors in splendid robes arrived at the shepherd's hut and asked the shepherd king for his daughter's hand. But when he had heard them out, the shepherd king frowned and asked them, "What is the prince's trade?"

The counsellors were astonished. "The prince does not need a trade," they told him. "He owns many lands and rich palaces and has all the money he requires."

"These are things that can change," said the shepherd king. "I will never marry my daughter to a man without a trade." And nothing the counsellors said would change his mind.

The prince was very cast down. "What can we do?" he asked his beloved. "Can you not persuade your father to think again?"

But the shepherd princess laughed. "My father is a very wise man," she said. "I think you had best learn a trade, my love, and as soon as possible."

The prince returned to the city and wandered through the market. He saw a blacksmith selling his wares for high prices. "Can you teach me your trade, blacksmith?" he asked.

"I can, my lord," said the blacksmith, "but you must be apprenticed for at least five years."

The prince could not wait so long. He went on to the stall of a carpenter whose furniture also fetched high prices. "Could you teach me your trade, carpenter?" he asked.

"If you will work hard for four years, my lord," said the carpenter, "I will teach you all I know."

The prince sighed, and moved on to the potter's stall, where the cheap jugs and bowls were finding ready buyers. "How long would it take me to learn to make pots?" he asked the potter.

"In a year or two," said the potter, "you could learn enough, my lord, to make a good living."

Once more the prince shook his head. He could not bear to wait so long to make the shepherd's daughter his bride.

Then he noticed an old woman who sat making a mat beside her stall. For her wares there were many buyers, because her prices were low. The prince greeted the old woman and asked her, "How long would it take me, Mother, to learn your trade?"

The old woman smiled up at him. "With your nimble young fingers, my lord," she said, "I could teach you in less than a week!"

The prince laughed aloud. "Make good your promise," he told her, "and

you shall never want for anything again!" So the old woman taught the prince how to make a mat. And when the week was up, the prince had made a mat that was good enough to sell. He gave the old woman more gold than she earned in a year, and rolling up his mat, carried it on his shoulder to the shepherd's hut.

The shepherd king and his daughter came out to meet him. The prince proudly unrolled his mat and laid it at his beloved's feet. She was delighted, and even the shepherd king was impressed.

"How long did it take you to make it?" he asked.

"Well, my first efforts weren't very good," the prince admitted, "but once I had mastered the skill, I made this one in a day."

"How much did it cost to make?" asked the shepherd king.

"Ten pence," said the prince.

"And what will you sell it for?"

"Twenty pence," the prince told him.

Then the shepherd king gave a deep sigh. "If only I had known of this trade," he said, "I should not have stayed a shepherd all these years!" And he gave his consent for the prince to marry his daughter.

When the wedding was over, the shepherd king decided to tell the prince's parents of their new daughter-in-law's royal birth. The king and queen were astonished to find that a king had lived so long as a shepherd in their land. "Why, your kingdom and ours have been friends for years now," they told him, "and your people still pray for your return!"

They gave the shepherd king a fine ship and a crew to sail him safely back to his own land, where his people welcomed him with great rejoicing.

The shepherd princess and her prince lived together in great happiness. The mat that the prince had made always took pride of place in the royal palace and was treasured by the couple above all their rich carpets. And when, in time, they had children of their own, each one was taught a useful trade – just in case!

The Most Beautiful Flower

Slovenia

Long ago there lived a prince who hated his father. The two of them were always quarrelling and the king would give his son no part in ruling the kingdom.

The prince married and had a daughter of his own, but he found his life tedious. He had nothing useful to do and could only bide his time, while his father grew older and ever more cantankerous.

At last the old king died and the prince, who had now reached middle age, suddenly found himself a king with great power. Unfortunately, he had neither the wisdom nor the experience to use his power well.

The first thing he did was to send out a decree that all the old people in the kingdom must leave within a week, or else they would be killed. "Old people are useless," he announced. "They stand in the way of younger men with new ideas."

Soon the roads of the kingdom were clogged with old people fleeing for the shelter of neighbouring lands. A week later, there was not an old man or woman to be seen throughout the length and breadth of the kingdom. Then soldiers were sent out to search for any who might be hiding, to kill them and anyone who had sheltered them.

"Now," said the king, "my land is free of old fools, and we shall all be the better for it!"

But unknown to the king, one old man still remained.

There was a young farmer whose parents had died when he was a child and who had been brought up by his grandfather. The old man had taught him all he knew about growing crops and caring for animals. The young farmer loved the old man and valued his wisdom, so he hid him in a big empty water-barrel. When the soldiers came to search, the farmer gave them his home-brewed ale to drink so that they grew drunk and careless and did not look in the barrel.

Years passed, and things did not go well in the kingdom. With no wise old counsellors to advise him, the king acted upon any whim which took his fancy, often with disastrous results. This was especially true when the time came to find a husband for his own daughter. He did not take the trouble to seek out young men of good family and character, from whom the princess could make her choice. Instead, he announced that all the young single men in the kingdom must come to the palace and the one who could best solve three riddles would be granted his daughter's hand in marriage. The princess was not pleased, but she knew it was useless to oppose her father's whims.

The farmer was one of the young men summoned to the palace and he returned that night to tell his old grandfather about the first riddle.

"We must all gather on a hill before daybreak," he said, "and guess the exact moment when the sun will rise."

The old man smiled. "All the other young men will look to the east, where the sun rises," he told his grandson. "But you must look westward to the high mountains. The moment you see the sun's first rays catch the top-most peak, you must cry 'Now!' for at that very instant the sun will rise into view in the east."

The young farmer did just as his grandfather had told him, and the king was delighted by his quickness. "Let us see how you fare with the next riddle," he said.

The young farmer went home and told his grandfather, "Tomorrow we must come into the king's presence 'wearing shoes and yet barefoot.'"

"Why, this is simple," said the old man, and taking a pair of his grandson's shoes, he carefully cut away the soles. From above, the shoes seemed whole, but beneath them the young man's feet were on the ground.

Most of the other suitors arrived next day with one shoe on and one shoe off. A few even turned up in their socks, but the king judged that the young farmer was the only one who had solved the riddle correctly.

But when the young man was given the third task, he returned in a state of deepest gloom. "This time," he told his grandfather, "we must bring to the princess the flower which in all the world smells best and looks most beautiful. Richer men will seek far and wide for the most exotic blooms, while I can choose only from the wild flowers that grow around the farm."

But the old man just laughed. He gave his grandson a single ear of wheat to take to the princess, and told him what to say to her.

Next morning, the steps of the palace looked like a vast florist's shop. The other young men had spent all they had on the most colourful scented blooms they could buy. The princess was growing quite bored sniffing them all.

When the young farmer presented her with a single ear of wheat, she raised her eyebrows in astonishment.

The king frowned. "What is this?" he demanded angrily. "Do you think my daughter merits no better gift than an ear of wheat?"

"I am a simple farmer, your majesty," said the young man, "and I have brought the princess the loveliest flower I know. There is nothing more beautiful to look upon than a field of golden wheat rippling in the wind, and nothing smells better than a wheat loaf fresh from the oven."

"He is right, Father!" said the princess, laughing, and the king nodded.

"It is true, indeed," he said, "and if you will have him, daughter, he shall be your husband and rule after me."

The princess agreed, for she liked the look of the young farmer. They walked back into the palace together and as they went, the king asked the young man how he came to have so much wisdom at so young an age.

The farmer hesitated, fearing the king's wrath if he told the truth. Then, plucking up his courage, he confessed how he had hidden his old grandfather because of his great love for him and because the old man had always given him such good advice.

The king frowned, and thought for a while before he spoke. He had begun to see that he would soon grow old himself, and he wanted a son-in-law who would love and respect him when that time came. What better choice could he make, he thought, than one who had risked his own life, for love of his old grandfather?

"I see now," he told the young couple, "that the wisdom of old people is something to be valued."

Then the king gave orders that all the old people who had fled the land could return and would be treated with great honour. So wisdom came back into the land, and from that day on, the people flourished.

The Chatterer

Russia

On the edge of a great forest, there lived an old man and his wife.

The man worked hard. He grew vegetables in his garden; he trapped the rabbits that came to steal his crops; and he caught fish in the river nearby. The old man and his wife never went hungry. But at night the old man lay awake in the darkness worrying about what would become of them when he grew too old and frail for these tasks, for they had never been rich enough to save any money.

"If only I had managed to put by a little store of gold," he thought, "then we should never go cold or hungry."

One day in the forest, gathering wood for their fire, he felt the ground give way beneath his feet. When he looked more closely, he saw that something hard lay beneath the ground. The old man knelt down and, tearing at the earth with his bare hands, found a small crock full of gold coins.

At first he could hardly believe his luck. Now he and his wife could face their last years without fear. But after he had feasted his eyes on his find, the old man put the crock of gold back into the hole and covered it again with clods of earth. Then he sat down and thought for a long time.

First, he thought that he might not be able to keep his treasure. The forest belonged to a rich lord who was known to be a miserly, greedy man. "If he finds out, he will never let us keep any of it," thought the old man. "I must take it home and hide it away. Then, if we spend it sparingly, no one need ever know."

But then he thought of a second problem. He loved his wife, but she was a hopeless chatterbox, gossiping to her neighbours about everything that happened to her or to her husband. She will never keep a secret like this, he thought sadly, and then all our gold will be taken from us.

For a long time the old man pondered. Then at last his face broke into a smile. He took a rabbit from one of his traps and a fish from his net. He tied the fish to a branch and, putting the dead rabbit into his fishnet, lowered it into the stream. Then he went home to his wife.

As they sat over their evening meal, the old man sighed.

"Why do you sigh, Husband?" asked his wife.

"I have a great secret," said the old man, "which I long to share with you."

"Tell me at once!" said the wife eagerly.

"But you might tell our neighbours," said her husband, "and then our good fortune would be lost to us."

"Good fortune?" exclaimed the old woman, desperate to hear the news. "I will never breathe a word of it!"

But the husband just shook his head mournfully.

The old woman seized the family bible. "I will take my oath on the Good Book," she said, "never to tell a living soul!"

"There is no need to swear it, Wife," he said. "I will trust to your promise." And he told her about his find.

"A pot of gold!" shrieked his wife. "And have you left it in the forest for another to steal? Quick, quick, Husband! Leave your meal and let us bring our treasure home."

But the old man sat slowly finishing his food, while his wife flew about like a bluebottle in her eagerness to be gone.

The light was fading as they set out. At the edge of the forest the old man paused and stood gazing up into a tree.

"What ails you?" asked his wife impatiently.

"I see a fish in that tree that would make us a good breakfast," said the old man.

"Oh, bother the fish!" said his wife. "We shall not need it once we have the gold." But her husband cut down the fish and put it in his sack.

When they reached the river, the husband paused again and gazed down into the water.

"What is it now?" demanded the old woman.

"I seem to have caught a rabbit in my fishnet," said the old man. "It will make a good stew for tomorrow's dinner."

"Oh, pooh to your rabbit!" exclaimed his wife. "We can buy good beef when we have gold to spend!" But the old man made her wait while he pulled up the net and put the rabbit safely away.

They came at last to the place where the pot was buried, and the old man dug it up. His wife was overjoyed, running the gold coins through her fingers, and as they went home she chattered on about how they would spend them. By now it was dark, and the wife grew nervous when a wolf howled in the distance. She clung to her husband in fear, but he only laughed.

"Let's hope it's our landlord," he muttered, "being carried off by the devil!"

When they reached home, the old man hid the pot of gold behind some loose bricks in the fireplace. "We must keep it for when we grow frail," he told his wife. "If we spend it now, the news of our riches will spread and our landlord will hear of it. Then he will come and take away our treasure."

But, try as she might, the old woman could not keep the secret, and when her husband wasn't looking she took a coin and bought herself a new bonnet. When the other wives admired it, she told them about the gold and made them promise not to tell anyone else.

But of course they did.

When the old man saw that the secret was out, he took the pot from its hiding-place without telling his wife, and buried it in his vegetable garden.

Word spread, until at last it reached the ears of the greedy landlord. He came riding up to the cottage on his fine horse and thumped on the door. Trembling, the old woman let him in.

"Where is this pot of gold?" roared the landlord. "It was found on my land and it belongs to me!"

"A pot of gold, my lord?" said the old man. "I know nothing of any pot of gold."

"Do not try to deceive me," said the landlord, narrowing his eyes. "Your wife has told everyone of your find."

The old man smiled. "My wife has strange dreams, my lord, and believes that they are true," he said.

The landlord hesitated. He turned to the old woman.

"Tell me about this gold," he ordered her. "Keep nothing back, or I shall have you locked in my cellar with the rats."

The old woman was very frightened. She began to babble nervously, "Well, my lord, we went through the forest and found a fish growing on a tree, and then we came to the river and stopped to take up a rabbit from our fishnet…"

The landlord frowned. He glanced at the old man, who sighed and shook his head sadly.

"Then we found a pot of gold and dug it up," went on the wife, "and as we came home, I was frightened by your lordship howling as you were carried off by the devil…"

The landlord was furious. "Do I look as if I have been carried off by the devil?" he shouted. "Fish in trees? Rabbits in the river? I've never heard such nonsense! And where is this gold now?"

Shaking with fear, the old woman pointed to the loose bricks. But when the landlord pulled them out, he found nothing but an old purse with a few small coins in it.

"Foolish woman, you have wasted my time!" said the angry landlord. He stamped out of the house, rode away on his fine horse, and never bothered the old couple again.

The man kept the gold safely hidden from his wife until a day came when they really needed it. As for the wife, she was never quite sure whether or not she had dreamed the whole thing, but she comforted herself that at least she had gained a new bonnet.

The Happy Man

Croatia

There was once a king who grew old and sick. He knew that he was close to death, but he was very powerful and could not believe that death would get the better of him. He called for all the best doctors in his kingdom and when they could not heal him, he sent for others in lands beyond the seas. But it was no use: he was dying of old age and for that, they told him, there was no cure.

Then word reached the king of a wise man in a land far away who knew the answer to everything. At once he sent messengers to ask the wise man how he could be cured.

The messengers returned and said, "Your Majesty must find a man who wants for nothing in this world. Take that man's shirt and put it on, and at once Your Majesty will be cured."

The old king was delighted. "I feel better already!" he told his counsellors, and he sent them to search throughout the kingdom for just such a man. The counsellors looked far and wide and found many rich and happy men. But always, when they questioned them, each could think of something that he still lacked which would have made his life complete.

While the counsellors travelled on into ever more distant lands, the old king grew weaker and weaker. Then, as they paused one night at a country inn, the counsellors heard a cheery, red-faced man talking loudly over a pint of ale in the corner by the fire. He seemed quite poor in his patched jacket and worn trousers. And yet he thumped his fist on the table and boasted loudly, "I want for nothing in this world!"

When they heard this, the counsellors surrounded him, begging him to come with them to save their king. "He will make you rich beyond your wildest dreams!" they promised.

"But I am rich enough already," said the man happily. "I have everything I need, so why should I travel all that way to see your old king?" Nothing could persuade him, and the counsellors were in despair. The very fact that they could not budge him with their bribes convinced them that here

indeed was the man they sought. In the end, they kept refilling the man's ale mug until he fell into a drunken stupor. Then they bundled him into their carriage and drove as fast as they could to the old king's palace.

They carried the drunken man into the king's presence. "At last, Your Majesty," they said, "we have found a man who is perfectly happy and who wants nothing more!"

The old king stretched out a feeble hand. "Give me his shirt," he croaked, "that I may put it on and be well again." As fast as they could, the counsellors tore off the man's patched jacket. But beneath it they found only a dirty, worn and tattered vest.

"Oh, your Majesty," stammered the counsellors. "It would seem that this happy fool has no shirt!"

When he heard this, the old king gave a long, pitiful groan and died at last. Only then did his counsellors understand the words of the wise man. For no man in all the world has everything he wants, and even kings cannot live for ever.

The Hundred Children

Romania

There once lived a man named Bukur who was famed for his strength and his cleverness. A cheerful, friendly man, he worked hard and planned well so that his farm prospered.

Bukur took for his wife a lively, pretty woman named Mara. Loving to one another and generous to their neighbours, they lived at peace with all the world. And yet there was sadness in their lives, for as the years passed no child was born to them.

Then one day, as he walked home from the fields, Bukur came upon a frail old man sitting by the roadside.

"Lean upon my arm, Father," said Bukur. "I will take you to my home where my good wife will feed you and give you a bed for the night."

The old man smiled. "Though I look old and frail," he said, "there is nothing I need. But you, with youth and strength, have sadness in your eyes."

Bukur sat down beside him. "You speak the truth, old Father," he said, "for though my wife and I live happily, there is always one blessing that is denied us."

"What is it you wish for?" asked the old man.

Bukur sighed. "A child," he said.

"You shall have one," said the old man. "And what else?"

Bukur smiled. "Only children," he said. "Nothing more."

"You shall have them," said the old man. "But what else?"

"What more could we want?" asked Bukur. "If we had children filling our house with their games and laughter, our lives would be complete." He smiled as he thought of the children playing, and glanced sideways at the old man. But to his astonishment, he found that there was no one there.

Bukur hurried home to tell Mara of his strange encounter. As he drew close to the farmhouse, he saw children running in and out of the doors and climbing in and out of

the windows. Hardly able to believe his eyes, he began to run and found Mara in the midst of the children. She looked up, laughing and crying all at once.

"First there was one," she told her husband, "then three or four, and then, suddenly, the whole house was full of children!"

It took a long time to sort them out and feed them all, and it was not until they lay asleep on the floor that Bukur and Mara could even begin to count them.

"A hundred children!" said Mara, her eyes still wide with astonishment.

"Is it too many?" asked Bukur anxiously, realising, too late, that he should have given more thought to his wishes. But Mara laughed and kissed him. "We have love enough for all of them," she said, "and you, I think, have strength and wisdom enough to feed even a hundred little mouths."

But it was not easy. Bukur worked harder than ever, building extra rooms and making a hundred little beds. Mara cooked from morning to night, but with a hundred extra mouths the food from the farm was not enough, and the children began to grow hungry.

"There is nothing else for it," said Bukur. "I must go out into the world and seek our fortune."

He hugged each child in turn, kissed Mara goodbye, and shouldering his pack, set off into the forest.

Many a long mile he walked and as night fell, reached a clearing where a huge flock of sheep were penned for the night.

The shepherds offered him shelter in their simple hut. "It is not safe to be out after dark," they told him, "for every night a dragon comes and steals three of our sheep."

"Can't you stop him?" asked Bukur, but the shepherds shook their heads. "It has been so," they said, "for as long as we can remember." Bukur thought about it as he gazed into the fire. Then he asked, "If I could stop this dragon from taking your sheep, would you give me some of your flock to help feed and clothe my family?" And he told them the story of his hundred children.

"Well," said the oldest shepherd, "if we gave you ten sheep for every child, it would be no more than the dragon steals in a single year."

"It would be a small price to pay," added another, "to be rid of his thieving for ever!"

A thousand sheep! thought Bukur, and he pictured Mara's delight when he drove them home. "I will do it!" he declared. "Tonight, when the dragon comes, I will go and challenge him."

When the dragon came, the ground trembled and the sheep bleated in fear. Bukur went out into the darkness and his courage almost failed him when he saw how big the dragon was. But he thought of his hungry children and said boldly, "I am Bukur the Strong, and you shall steal no more sheep from this flock."

The dragon was taken aback: for all his size he was really rather stupid.

"How will you stop me?" asked the dragon. "I am bigger and stronger than you are."

Bukur laughed. "I doubt it!" he said. "Why, I am so strong, I can squeeze water from a stone." And he took a big lump of Mara's fresh cheese from his pack and squeezed it until the whey ran down his fingers.

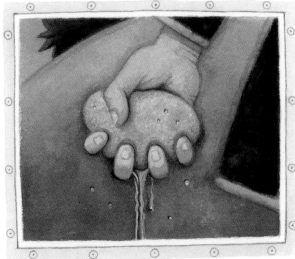

The dragon had never seen cheese, and was alarmed by this show of strength. He stood and hesitated.

Now, as it happened, the dragon's mother was seeking a strong servant to fetch and carry for her. The dragon thought he could get Bukur away from the sheep and please his mother at the same time.

"If you will come and work for my mother," he told Bukur, "she will give you gold for your pains."

Bukur knew that dragons always have a big hoard of gold, so he agreed to go.

When they reached the dragon's cave, the mother looked at Bukur and snorted. "He doesn't look very strong," she said. "Let's see how far he can throw your iron club."

The club was so big and heavy that Bukur doubted whether he could even lift it. "You throw it first," he told the dragon, "and then I will throw it further." The dragon threw the club right out of sight, and they found it a mile away.

"Now it is your turn," said the dragon.

Bukur shook his head. "I shall wait until moonrise," he said. "Then I shall throw it right over the moon."

The dragon frowned. "What if it falls short?" he said. "It might land on the moon and I should lose it for ever."

"That would be a sad loss," agreed Bukur, "but I must prove my strength to your mother."

The dragon did not want to lose his club. "I'll throw it back," he told Bukur, "and tell her that you threw it." Bukur agreed, and the dragon threw the club back. But the dragon's mother still had her doubts.

Next day she gave them each a buffalo skin and told them to fetch water from the well. It was a long way away, and Bukur knew that he could never carry the huge skin full of water. He took a spade from his pack and began to dig around the well.

"I can't waste time with this tiny load," he told the dragon, "I'll dig up the whole well and carry that home."

The dragon was alarmed. "If you do that," he said, "the well may run dry. Leave it, and I will carry both waterskins home."

Next morning, the dragon's mother sent them both to fetch wood for the fire. The dragon tore up a whole oak tree and tossed it over his shoulder. Bukur took a rope from his pack.

"I can't be bothered with twigs," he said scornfully. "I'll tie my rope around the whole forest and drag that home."

"Stop!" cried the dragon. "Without the forest, no more trees will grow and we shall run out of firewood."

"But your mother needs wood now," said Bukur.

"I will take two trees," said the dragon, "one for each of us."

When they reached the cave, the dragon was sweating under his load while Bukur walked behind with his hands in his pockets. Then the dragon's mother realised that Bukur was too cunning for her foolish son.

"I must get rid of this man," she thought.

That night, Bukur heard the dragons plotting. "You must beat him to death while he sleeps," said the mother to her son.

Bukur took a log, put it under his blanket, and hid under the bed. The dragon came in the darkness and struck the log many violent blows. Then, leaving Bukur for dead, he went back to sleep.

Next morning, Bukur stretched and yawned. "I could hardly sleep last night," he said, "for the moths brushing against my face."

Now the dragons were really afraid. "What if he comes to us in the night and beats us to death?" said the mother. Her son trembled at the thought. "But he won't go," he said, "without the gold I promised him."

"Then we must pay him off," said the mother crossly.

She fetched a huge bag of gold from their secret hoard and offered it to Bukur.

"All this shall be yours," she said, "if you will go away and leave us in peace!"

Bukur looked thoughtful.

"I promised the shepherds," he said, "that your son would steal no more sheep from them."

"That is agreed," said the dragon's mother.

"Then I will go," said Bukur, "if your son will come with me to speak to the shepherds and help me carry the gold."

So Bukur and the dragon set off, and when they reached the sheepfold, the dragon promised that he would never steal from the flock again.

The grateful shepherds gave Bukur a thousand sheep and he drove them home while the dragon followed, carrying the gold.

As they came in sight of the farmhouse, the children saw them and came running in a great crowd towards their beloved father.

The dragon stopped in his tracks. He had never seen so many children all waving and shouting.

"Why are they so excited?" he asked.

"Oh, well," said Bukur, "It is just that roast dragon is their favourite food, and I promised I would try to find one for them."

The dragon was terrified. As the children drew close, he dropped the bag of gold, and running as fast as he could, vanished into the far distance.

And from that day Bukur and Mara lived well and happily with their flock of sheep and the dragons' gold – and their hundred children never went hungry again.

Sources

The Twelve Months
Slovakia
Prostonarodnie slovenske povesti,
Pavol Dobsinsky
(Turc.sv.Martin 1880-1883)

Misery
Poland
Powiesci I opowiadania
ludowe z okolic Przasnysza,
collected by Stanislaw
Chelchowski (Warszawa 1889)

The Shepherd King
Serbia
Srpske narodne pripovijetke,
V.S. Karadzic
(Beograd, 1928)

The Most Beautiful Flower
Slovenia
Slovenske Narodne Pravljice in
Pripovedke, B. Krek
(Lubljana, 1885)

The Chatterer
Russia
Narodnyje russkije skazki
I-III, A. Afanasjev
(Moscow, 1958, based on
1st edition 1855-1863)

The Happy Man
Croatia
Narodne Pravljice in Legende,
Manica Komanova
(Lubljana 1923)

The Hundred Children
Romania
Povesti ardelenesti culese din gura
poporului de …,
Ion Pop-Reteganul (Brasov, 1913)